WHO HAS SEEN THE
BEAST?

ANNE SCHRAFF

PAGETURNERS®

SADDLEBACK
EDUCATIONAL PUBLISHING
www.sdlback.com

ISBN: 978-1-68021-382-9
eBook: 978-1-63078-783-7

Printed in the United States
25 24 23 22 21   2 3 4 5 6

PAGETURNERS® | ADVENTURE

Chapter 1

Lettie Marin and her parents had been planning a camping trip to Owl Lake for the past year. It was meant to be a family celebration. Lettie would be graduating from high school. Her brother, Jacob, would be finishing up two years of community college. Now it was late June. At last the family was headed for the mountains in their rented RV. Dad was in the driver's seat, carefully rounding each curve of the steep, winding road.

"I hope we get a decent campsite," he said. "We probably won't be by the lake, though. You have to reserve those spots early. I should have called a lot sooner."

The campground was just ahead. Dad

slowed and turned onto the dirt road. He drove toward the lake, hoping they might see an open spot. It looked like a family was packing up to leave. They were hurriedly loading their gear into a van. Could it be possible? The spot was perfect. It was a beautiful, isolated campsite. There was a clear view of the lake through the pine trees.

"Are you leaving?" Dad called out.

A man looked up. He had a grim look on his face. "Yeah. We sure are," he said. "You're welcome to this place!"

Mom laughed. "It looks as though someone just remembered they left the stove on back home."

"This is great!" Jacob said.

"Wow!" Lettie said as she looked around. "I can even see snow on the mountain peaks. This is like paradise." She was too distracted to notice the panicked campers.

The van backed up and spun around. Now the Marins could see that the family had left some things behind. There were two sleeping bags and an ice chest.

"Hey!" Dad yelled at the driver. "You left your—"

He was cut off mid-sentence. "Keep it," the man called back. "We're out of here."

By now Mom was no longer laughing. She was concerned by this family's reaction. "What's the matter?" she called out to the man. "Did something bad happen?"

"Bad? Yeah, you could say that. There's something really bad going on in those woods," he said. Then the van sped forward, tires screeching and gravel flying. In seconds it had vanished.

Jacob laughed. "Talk about stressed out."

Dad backed the RV into the campsite.

"That's too bad," Mom said. "I can't imagine wanting to give up this spot. But for some reason they felt they had to."

"A skunk probably came out of the

woods and scared them," Jacob said. "Some people aren't used to being out in the wild. It could have been anything that freaked them out. I'm just glad we were the ones to get this place. I can't wait to go fishing."

"And I can't wait to take pictures," Lettie said. "Look how the water sparkles. It's like the lake is covered in diamonds."

The Marin family had been coming to Owl Lake for years. Lettie and Jacob had good memories of this place. They'd had nothing but fun here. The family couldn't imagine anything bad happening.

Jacob pulled the fishing gear from the RV. "Get ready, everybody! Tonight we're having trout for dinner."

"Cooked over an open flame," Mom said. "I can't wait."

Dad was focused on the woods. "I bet there's a lot of wildlife around," he said. "I'm hoping to see some deer."

"Ooh. Maybe we'll see a bear," Lettie

said. "I bet there's one checking us out right now from behind all those trees. He's thinking about dinner." She laughed.

"Actually, we do need to be careful," Mom said. "Bears know when there's food around. And they'll come right up to a campsite to get it. So let's not leave anything out."

"That might be what scared those people away," Dad said. "Maybe they were hiking in the woods and a bear chased them. I could see how that would be a bad thing."

"Well, something scared them," Mom agreed. "No one would leave behind such nice gear unless there was a good reason."

"Did you see what they left on the picnic table?" Jacob said. "It's a knife. A really good one. It'll be perfect for cleaning the—" Jacob took a step backward. "Whoa! There's blood on it."

Chapter 2

That's disgusting!" Lettie said as she looked down at the bloody knife. "Keep that thing away from me."

"I'm sure it's no big deal," Dad said. "The knife was probably used to gut some fish. Or maybe someone accidentally cut themselves."

"*Please* get rid of it," Lettie said to her father.

"I know what to do," he said. Dad used a paper towel to pick up the knife. Then he dropped it into a plastic bag. "I'm sure those people aren't coming back any time soon. But we can take all their stuff to the ranger station."

Lettie had started to wonder about the blood. "Hey, Dad," she said. "Do you think some kind of creature tried to attack those people?" she asked.

Jacob was laughing. "Yeah," he said. "Like one of those beasts that's half-human, half-ape. I've heard the woods are full of them. They hide out during the day. At night they chase people. I just hope they don't eat the trout."

Now Lettie was laughing too. It did sound ridiculous. But then her voice became more serious.

"Well, I know there are stories about a creature like that. The Yeti. Some people say they've seen it."

"That's the one that lives in the mountains of Asia," Jacob said. "The creature that's supposed to live around here is Bigfoot."

"Stop, Jacob," Dad said, chuckling. "You're going to scare your sister. You know none of that is real. Anyone who has claimed to see Bigfoot is either joking or they have really bad eyesight. It's just some kind of animal they've seen. Like a bear. Now let's set up camp."

"After that I'm going fishing," Jacob said. "I have to catch our dinner."

"Why don't you help me set up a cooking area," Mom said to Jacob. "Lettie, you help your father with the other gear."

Soon the campsite was ready. Lettie and Jacob headed for Owl Lake. Jacob carried the fishing gear. Lettie had her new digital camera. Cell phone pictures were good. But she could do more with the new camera. It had a better zoom feature and a slower speed for night pictures. And there was no limit to how many photos she could take. Lettie wanted to capture every detail of this trip.

"You don't think Bigfoot is real, do you?" Lettie asked as they walked.

Jacob shrugged. "Not really. But some people say they've seen him. Grandpa says he did once. He was camping in Northern

California near the coast. He saw a big hairy beast walk into the forest."

They had reached the lake. Jacob got ready to fish. He was baiting his hook. Lettie aimed her camera at him and snapped a picture. She looked at the photo. The image was sharp and clear. The colors were bright. It would be great to get a picture of a deer. Her dad would love that. Lettie walked around taking more pictures.

After about an hour she checked with Jacob. He had caught enough fish for dinner. It was time to head back to the campsite. "I can't wait to show Mom and Dad the photos I took," Lettie said.

Mom was putting wood on the campfire when Jacob and Lettie walked up. "Look at these, Mom." Lettie held the camera in front of her.

"These are great photos, Lettie," she said looking at the screen. "This close-up of the mountains is incredible. It's like you were standing right there next to them. And look how blue—Wait. What's this?" she asked.

"What?" Lettie said, looking over her mother's shoulder.

"Look. Right there near the woods."

"It could be a bear. But it's so tall," Lettie said. "Maybe it's standing on its hind legs. Or it might just be a shadow."

"Let me see," Dad said. He looked closely at the photo. "If I didn't know better, I'd say it was Bigfoot." The rest of the family looked over at him.

"Ed!" Mom said to her husband.

That's when he smiled. "I think Lettie is right. It's just a shadow."

Just then a truck pulled up near the campsite. "Hi," a voice called out. Ed Marin turned to look. A young guy was leaning out the window. "You got a great spot," he said.

Dad walked toward him, smiling. "It's perfect. Private and so quiet. We got lucky," he said. "My family is going to have a great week here. I'm Ed Marin, by the way."

The guy had gotten out of his truck. "Nice to meet you, Mr. Marin. I'm Kyle Ward," he said. "My parents own the rental cabins down the road. We have a restaurant too."

"Hi, Kyle. Do you happen to know anything about the people who were here before us?"

"They'd been here for only a day," Kyle said. "I guess something really scared them." He looked away for a moment. Then he continued. "Their story didn't make much sense. Supposedly one of their sons was attacked. Some kind of beast did it, they said. The father used a knife to scare it away."

Ed was thinking back to something his kids had said earlier. They were joking about a beast.

Kyle shook his head. "Some people get scared by the littlest things. It could be just a noise or a shadow. Their imaginations run wild."

Chapter 3

What about the blood?" Ed asked Kyle. "That was real. I would think the ranger or the sheriff would have gotten involved. Even if the story was farfetched. I know I'd call someone for help."

"The sheriff did speak to the family," Kyle said. "But they couldn't give him any real facts. They just kept insisting that the attacker was half-human, half-ape. It came out of the woods and grabbed one of their kids. This campground has been here for decades. No one has ever reported seeing any kind of beast. The sheriff decided it wasn't worth investigating. He didn't have enough officers anyway."

Lettie walked up beside her father. She wondered what the two men were talking about. Secretly she wanted to know who this guy was. He was really good-looking, she thought. And he seemed nice too. Before now, she wouldn't have noticed him. She'd had a boyfriend. But they broke up a couple of months ago. Now she was curious. Was the guy close to her age? Would he like to hang out? It was fun to think about, even if nothing happened between them.

Dad and Kyle had finished their conversation. Lettie hadn't heard much of what they'd said. Now Kyle smiled and got back into his truck.

"Remember," Kyle said. "The restaurant is here if you need it. We make a great picnic lunch. It's perfect for taking on a hike. Or you might just want to sit down for a meal."

"Sounds good," Dad said.

Kyle waved as he drove away.

Back at the campfire, Jacob was getting ready to fry the fish. Dad walked over to him. "That was quite a catch you made, son."

Mom was busy arranging food on the picnic table. Lettie stepped away to look at the scenery. To her, this was the most beautiful spot on earth. It was impossible to imagine anything sinister happening here.

Soon the family sat down to eat. They talked about the day's events, laughing at the idea of a big hairy beast being somewhere nearby. Now the sun was going down. It gave a pink glow to the snow on the mountain peaks. Then the sun disappeared. The stars looked bright against the dark sky. They seemed close enough to touch.

"Tomorrow I want to go for a hike," Mom said. "I read that there are over forty species of birds in this area. I'd like to see as many as possible."

"A hike sounds good," Dad said.

Jacob stood up. "I think I'll take a walk,"

he said. "Maybe I'll see some raccoons or an opossum."

"Be careful, Jacob. Yeti might be lurking in the woods just waiting to grab you," Lettie said, half-jokingly.

"I told you. Yeti lives in the Himalayas." Jacob laughed. "It's Bigfoot we have to watch out for."

"Oh, right," Lettie said, rolling her eyes.

She watched as her brother left the campsite. Now it was very quiet. Her parents had already gone to bed. Lettie decided to sit outside a while longer. It was such a refreshing change from being at home. There was so much noise and pollution in the city. Here there was only the sound of the wind rustling through the trees. The air smelled fresh and clean. Lettie loved the smell of pine trees. She took a deep breath.

Suddenly there was a noise. It sounded like a twig snapping. Startled, Lettie looked around. It must have been Jacob returning, she hoped. All the talk about Bigfoot and Yeti had planted a tiny seed of fear in her mind. Of course she didn't really believe that a half-human, half-ape was roaming through the woods. But …

"How was your walk, Jacob?" Lettie called out into the darkness. "Did you see any raccoons or opossums?"

There was no answer. But Lettie heard a rattling sound coming from the other side of the RV. "Jacob?" she called out again. A chill went down her spine. Then she remembered what her mother had said about bears. They'll come right up to a campsite if there's food around.

It had to be a bear, Lettie told herself. She now wished she was safe inside the RV with her parents. To get inside, though, she'd have to walk to the other side of the RV. That's where the strange noise was coming from. Lettie wasn't sure what to do. Stay right there? Run for the door to the RV?

Either way, she could end up being dinner for a hungry bear.

"Is it you, Jacob?" she called out one more time. Again there was no answer. But now the sounds had stopped. She had to make a move.

Lettie walked to the back of the RV. She leaned over and peered around the corner. The path was clear. Lettie made a run for it. She grabbed the handle and yanked the door open. Now she was inside and safe. She tried to catch her breath. That's when there was another noise. Lettie held her breath so she could hear. What was it?

Chapter 4

Could Jacob be playing a practical joke? He did that a lot when he was younger. Lettie thought he'd grown out of that type of behavior. But he had been teasing her earlier about Bigfoot.

Suddenly there was a crash. It had come from outside. She peeked out a window. Two chairs had fallen over. "Mom! Dad!" she shouted. The two of them came out of their room.

"What's up?" her father asked, looking sleepy and confused.

"There's something going on!" Lettie said. "I've been hearing strange noises. And just now two chairs fell over."

"Okay. Try to calm down. I'll check

it out," he said, grabbing a flashlight. He reached for the door.

"Wait," she said suddenly. Whatever was outside could be really dangerous. Lettie was afraid for herself and her family. And that wasn't normally like her.

"It's okay, honey," he said, trying to reassure his daughter. "You have to remember that we're out in nature. There are all kinds of creatures here. And there are bound to be strange noises. It doesn't mean there's danger. It's like when we went to visit Grandpa in the Philippines. We were scared when we first heard the long-tailed monkeys. Remember how they screeched? It was a frightening sound. But we weren't in any danger. It's just that we'd never heard anything like that."

Lettie smiled at the memory of visiting the Philippines. It was the place her ancestors had come from. She loved the culture and the customs. Now she was feeling a little foolish. "You're right, Dad. I'm sure it's nothing."

"I'll look around anyway," he said.

There was nothing unusual outside the RV. But Mom had become concerned about Jacob. "He should be back from his walk by now," she said.

"You know how our son is. He finds something that interests him. Then he loses all track of time."

"But he said he would be right back, Ed. I just hope he's not lost," Mom said. "Jacob might think he knows his way around. But it's been a few years since we've been here. I'm really getting worried."

"Wait!" Lettie said. She had spotted a shadow in the distance. It was coming toward the RV. "Isn't that Jacob? I think he's coming now."

"Thank goodness!" Mom said with relief.

"Look how slowly he's walking," Lettie said. "Something must be wrong."

The family ran across the meadow to meet Jacob.

"Jacob!" Lettie cried. "Are you okay? Your shirt is torn. And you look like you've been in a fight. What happened out there?"

"It's kind of a blur," Jacob said. "I was following some raccoon tracks. Then something heavy came down on my head and I fell."

"Jacob!" Mom cried, putting her arms around him. "It looks like something has been clawing at your shirt. And you've got deep scratches on your arms!"

"Do you think maybe a branch fell on your head?" Dad asked. He was trying not to sound alarmed. "I mean, you don't think you were attacked, do you?"

"I'm not sure," Jacob said, holding his hand to his head. "It all happened so fast. I guess it could have been a branch. But I had the feeling that someone … or something … was clawing at me."

There was a little bit of blood in Jacob's hair. And he had the scratches on his arms. It didn't seem like his injuries were too serious. Still, Dad would have to call the sheriff. The people who'd been there before them reported being attacked. But no one believed them. Now maybe someone would listen. "There could be some kind of stalker out here," Dad said. "Something needs to be done about it."

The sheriff and an ambulance arrived quickly. The paramedics gave Jacob first aid. His wounds were minor, they said. But he might want to go to the hospital just in case.

Jacob looked at his father. "I'm not spending my vacation in the ER," he said firmly. "I'm fine."

Dad spoke to the paramedics. They told him the signs to watch for. A bad headache or dizziness. Bleeding from the nose or mouth. "Call us immediately if your son has any of these symptoms."

The sheriff interviewed Jacob. The questions came at him fast, one after the other. Who attacked you? Did you see a face? Were any words spoken by the person?

Jacob was shaking his head. "I just don't know what happened," he said.

"It's okay, honey," Mom said.

Dad walked up beside his wife and Jacob.

"So you were walking in the woods," the sheriff recounted from his notes. "You followed some raccoon tracks. Then you were hit on the head and fell. You're not sure whether it was an animal or a person who attacked you." He looked up at Jacob and Dad. "It's not much to go on. But I've got your report. Let me know if you remember anything else."

Lettie had been nearby listening. She could tell the sheriff didn't believe Jacob. Why would he? He didn't believe the previous campers. That's what Kyle had said. The sheriff had thought they were hysterical. And now it seemed he thought Jacob was hysterical too.

The sheriff had left. Jacob was trying to figure out exactly what had happened.

"I was crouched down, looking at animal tracks," he said to his parents. "Then I stood up and hit my head on a tree branch. That makes the most sense. Of course I wasn't attacked by the Abominable Snowman. Did you see the way the sheriff looked at me?"

"Then why was your shirt ripped?" Mom asked.

"I don't know. Maybe some of the branches were sharp or had thorns on them," Jacob said in frustration.

"It could have been a bear," Dad said. "You shouldn't have been out there by yourself in the dark."

"Let's go to bed," Mom said. "We'll get a fresh start in the morning. Remember, we're going on a hike. Come on, Ed. Let's go inside."

Jacob was about to go inside too when Lettie tugged on his shirt.

"Bears don't hit people over the head," she said softly. "Only a person could do that. Or—"

"Or a half-human, half-ape?" Jacob said with a grin.

Jacob was restless the whole night. He noticed every little sound. His common sense told him it was only raccoons or opossums roaming around. But part of him wanted to believe a beast could be out there. It was kind of exciting. Think of the stories he could tell his friends. Finally Jacob fell asleep. He awoke to the smells of breakfast cooking.

Mom and Dad had finished eating. Lettie was putting on her hiking boots.

"Hurry up, Jacob," Lettie called inside to him. "We want to get going."

Jacob came out of the RV and quickly ate something.

"We're going to check out the trail you were on last night," Dad said. "Maybe we can find some clues."

The family set out on their hike. Jacob led them to the exact place where he had fallen. "Look here!" he called out. He was pointing to a button. "It's from my shirt," he said.

"I don't see any low branches," Lettie said, looking up into the trees.

"Come over here," Mom said. She was examining something on the ground. The area was damp because of a nearby stream. Tracks of some kind were imprinted in the mud. "Are these footprints?" she asked.

Jacob knelt beside his mother. "They look like the prints of someone who was walking barefoot," he said.

"Those are awfully big prints," Dad said.

The first thing Lettie thought of was Bigfoot. It sent a shiver down her spine.

"These footprints are over twelve inches long," Jacob said. "And look. There are two more footprints going the other way. Whatever it was must have gone back into the woods."

"It?" Dad repeated. "What are you saying, Jacob? Do you really believe some kind of creature attacked you?"

"No," Jacob said quickly. "But it is weird. Remember how I was joking about the mountain creature called Yeti? Well, I read this article. It said that five people were battered to death by yetis. This was in 1957. It happened in Asia. Some villagers had reported it."

"That can't be true," Mom said in disbelief. "I've heard of yetis. But I didn't think they really existed. Now you're telling me they've actually killed people?"

"It could have been something else that killed them," Jacob said. "But the article also told about someone else. A guy from

Norway was hiking in the Himalayas. He reported that a yeti attacked him. It nearly broke his shoulder. The man swore to it."

"Well, I know one thing," Dad said. "We're sticking together for the rest of this trip. No one goes out walking alone, okay? But we're not going to be driven out by something that probably doesn't exist."

Chapter 5

That night the Marins decided to eat at the restaurant. Dad wanted to try the food. The young man who had stopped by yesterday made it sound so good. Kyle's parents owned the restaurant and the cabins.

Kyle was working that night. He called out to the Marins when they entered the restaurant. "Nice to see you," he said as he seated them. "The special tonight is meatloaf. And my mother made her famous apple pie."

"Sounds great," Dad said.

Kyle gave the cook the orders. Then he returned to the table. "I heard something about another attack," he said.

Jacob told him what had happened the night before.

"That's really strange," Kyle said. "You must have been scared."

"Have you ever seen any kind of creatures around here?" Lettie asked. "Besides the normal ones, I mean."

"Like Bigfoot," Jacob said with a big smile as he nudged Lettie.

"No. I've never seen anything like that," Kyle said. "But as you know by now, some people have. Like the campers who had your spot. They claimed to have seen some kind of creature."

"But the people before them didn't have any problems, right?" Dad asked.

"Right. It was two young guys. They never left the campsite," Kyle said. "I remember they weren't very friendly. It seems they didn't have a lot of money. Their gear was in bad shape. And their car was beat up. But they were good campers. They kept the site neat."

"Well, I think I got knocked out by a tree branch. All this talk about Bigfoot is silly," Jacob said. "I'm feeling great now."

"Do you and your family live at Owl Lake?" Lettie asked Kyle.

"Yeah," he said. "We've been here since I was five. Now I'm eighteen."

Lettie looked surprised. This place was in the middle of nowhere. Where had Kyle gone to school?

Kyle saw the look on her face. He quickly explained. "I was homeschooled," he said. "College is going to be a big change."

The family finished their meal. They thanked Kyle and headed back to camp. That night they made plans for another hike.

The Marins headed out early the next morning. This time they avoided the area where Jacob had gotten hurt. It was a pleasant but tiring hike. The family was ready to relax. They walked up to their campsite.

Lettie called out, "Look! Somebody has been digging big holes around the RV!"

"And it looks like they tried to fill the holes back up," Jacob said.

"What is going on?" Mom asked, frowning.

Dad studied the fresh piles of loose dirt. "It seems like somebody was looking for something," he said.

"Like buried treasure?" Lettie asked. "That would be exciting."

"Yeah. That's it," Jacob said, rolling his eyes. "The ghosts of pirates are here scaring the campers away so they can dig in peace."

The Marins were staring at the holes. That's when a man walked up. He had curly gray hair. His beard was red. The man's face didn't look old. He didn't have any lines, just a dark suntan. A bandana was wrapped around his head. There was a walking stick in one hand. "Hello there," he called out. The family looked up, startled. He smiled cheerfully.

"Hello," Dad said.

The man reached out to shake Ed's hand. "My name is Siskin," he said. "I spend time traveling around these mountains. It looks like you've had a visitor."

"Giant gophers, you think?" Dad asked.

The man shook his head. "Nope. Gophers didn't do this," he said. "There's only one explanation."

"What is it?" Dad asked.

The man smiled. "UFOs."

"UFOs?" Jacob repeated in disbelief. He was trying hard not to laugh.

"Sure," Siskin said. "They've been in these mountains for a long time. They're taking soil samples. That's what you're seeing there. I have no doubt about it."

"What do the UFOs look like?" Lettie asked, also trying not to laugh.

"Oh, you know," Siskin said. "They're shaped like saucers. You've seen pictures of them, I'm sure. But lots of people have seen the real objects. The government tries to cover it up, though. A few of us have even seen the beings inside the ships. They're covered with white hair. They have thin lips and dark eyes."

Lettie glanced at her father. They were both thinking the same thing. Siskin was an odd character. But it might have been part of a plan. He looked like someone who loved the wilderness. And he probably wanted it to stay wild. All the visitors to the area only disturbed nature and damaged the environment. He must have made up this story, hoping to scare campers away.

Maybe it was Siskin who had hit Jacob over the head. Then he knocked over the chairs at the campsite. And who knows? Maybe it was Siskin who dug these holes.

Chapter 6

So tell me, Mr. Siskin," Ed said calmly. "Do you think there could be something special about this campsite? Some special reason the … uh … UFO guys might not want people camping here?"

"Yeah, sure," Siskin said. "Some places have special vibrations. Aliens are working underground. There are places like that in New Mexico. People know to leave these areas alone. This place is like that. It would be best if no one ever camped here."

"So you think we should move on?" Jacob asked.

"That's up to you," Siskin said with a serious look on his face. "You can take your chances. Who's going to stop you? But those aliens can get pretty aggressive. I've seen them work. They never bother me, of course. That's because I agree with them. The wilderness should be left alone." Then Siskin said goodbye and walked away.

"What a scam!" Dad laughed when the man was gone. "He would go to any extreme to keep people away from this place."

Jacob nodded. "Yeah. But I halfway agree with him. It bothers me to see all the trash people leave around. I even saw beer cans out in the meadow. Some deer were grazing right next to them."

"We're always careful not to litter," Lettie said.

"I know. But some people don't care. They show up here to go camping. There might be hundreds of campers at a time. And the wilderness gets trashed," Jacob said.

"But, honey," Mom said. "It's not right either to prevent people from enjoying such a beautiful place. Maybe there need to be stricter rules."

"Well, anyway," Dad said. "Now we have a good idea of who's been bothering us. Let's keep our eyes open. Siskin could be back to cause more trouble. In that case we'll need to call the sheriff."

Later that evening, Dad barbecued hamburgers and hot dogs. The family enjoyed their meal as they sat around a campfire. "What do you think guys? Isn't this relaxing?" their father asked.

The family told stories and roasted marshmallows before going to bed. It was midnight when the silence was shattered by a series of loud unearthly shrieks.

"What is that sound?" Mom cried out.

"It looks like old Siskin is up to no good again," Dad grumbled. "He's probably set up a loudspeaker. And now he's got the sound effects going. The man is crazy."

Lettie peered out the window. All she

saw was darkness. But the blood-curdling shrieks continued. She huddled under her blankets and thought about her comfortable bedroom at home. She finally understood why those other campers had taken off. Having a beautiful campsite with a view of Owl Lake was great. But it wasn't worth this nightly horror show.

"Let's just get out of here," Lettie groaned. "I'm sick of whatever is going on."

"I won't let Siskin chase us out of here," Dad exclaimed. "He's not going to ruin our vacation!"

The guys went outside with their flashlights. They pointed them toward the woods. That's where the shrieks seemed to be coming from. "Hey, Siskin," Dad shouted. "Stop what you're doing now! You aren't scaring anybody. You're just making a fool of yourself!"

Suddenly the shrieks stopped. Dad grinned. "We've caught him in the act. I think he's getting the message. I understand his concerns for nature. But this has to stop," he said.

Lettie was relieved. She had actually started to believe that some creature was waiting to attack them. But now her father's warning had put an end to the shrieking. There was no doubt that Siskin had been responsible.

Dad was still grinning when he came back inside the RV. "I've been standing up to bullies all my life," he said proudly. "There were always tough kids in school who picked on other kids. But I learned to stand up to the bullies. And they always backed down."

Lettie decided that there was no danger. The Yeti or Bigfoot was a fake. It was safe to go outside. She wanted to look at the stars and find her favorite constellations. Now was a good time since she was wide awake. She opened the door and stepped out.

Just then her mother saw her. "Come back inside, Lettie," she called. "We need to get back to sleep. Tomorrow we're going to hike around Eagle Mountain. And we're planning to leave early."

There was no chance for Lettie to respond. Someone had grabbed her and put a hand over her mouth. She tried to scream but no sound came out. Lettie was being dragged away. Her attacker held her tightly, leaving her helpless to fight.

"Please come in now!" She could still hear her mom calling out. "We've had enough excitement for one night."

Whoever had her was pulling her toward the woods. Or was it even a human? She could see that the arm around her was huge and hairy. It definitely did not look human!

This can't be happening, Lettie thought to herself. The creature she and Jacob had joked about was here at Owl Lake. Yeti? Bigfoot? It didn't matter. All Lettie knew was that the beast had her. And it was dragging her deeper and deeper into the woods!

Chapter 7

I *have to do something,* Lettie thought. That's when she kicked the beast as hard as she could. But it just kept moving. Then Lettie bit down on the hand clamped over her mouth. This time the beast reacted with a grunt. Still, it continued to drag her farther into the woods.

Why was this happening to her? Only a few days ago she had graduated from high school. She was looking forward to a great summer. First was the camping trip to the Sierras. And then she would go to the Philippines to visit her grandparents. Her life was really good. Suddenly it was all coming to an end.

It seemed impossible that such a hideous

creature could live in these beautiful mountains. It was harder to believe that no one knew about it. Not the park rangers. Not even the sheriff.

Lettie kicked the beast again. It let out a cry. The grip on Lettie's mouth loosened for a second. "Help!" she screamed. "Help!"

Now she could see the guys running toward her. They had already been out searching. Then they heard her scream.

The creature let go of her. She watched as it started to run. It was important to get a good description. Over six feet tall. Dark, tangled hair. Lettie had also noticed that the creature smelled bad. It had the odor of an old, moldy towel. Lettie kept watching until the creature disappeared.

"Sweetheart!" Dad said. "Are you okay?" He put his arms around his daughter and held her tight. He could feel her shaking in his arms.

"It was horrible, Dad," Lettie said.

"That thing came from out of nowhere and grabbed me. I was so afraid. But I tried to fight. It's scary to think about what could have happened."

"I can't believe this happened to you, sis," Jacob said. "It's crazy to think that a creature like Bigfoot could really be out here. I thought it was just a myth. Or a joke. Now I'm beginning to think that is what attacked us."

Mom came running toward them. She was out of breath. There was a look of fear on her face. "Is she okay? Is my baby okay? Oh, Lettie—"

"I'll be okay," Lettie assured her mother. "I kicked that thing as hard as I could. That's when it let me go and ran away. It doesn't seem like I'm hurt. But the smell of that nasty creature is all over me. I need a shower."

"You should be proud of yourself for fighting back," Jacob said.

Lettie smiled. "I do have a good kick," she said. "It's all that soccer I used to play."

"Well, we're not staying here," Dad said. "Not after this. It's not worth the safety of my family. We'll leave right after you get cleaned up, Lettie. Right now I'm going to call the sheriff. This time he had better do something about it!"

◆ ◆ ◆

The sheriff arrived at the campsite just after dawn. He took Lettie's statement. Then he and his deputy did a search for evidence. They didn't find anything. But at least they were taking this more seriously now.

"I've lived in this place for over forty years," the sheriff said. "I grew up in the foothills of these mountains. For eleven years now I've been sheriff. Not once have I seen evidence of a creature that could be called Bigfoot. Sure, there have been some wild stories. Mostly from campers who have had too much to drink. But nothing has ever convinced me it's true."

"Well, I saw it and it grabbed me," Lettie insisted. "I've never been so scared."

Jacob remembered something. Lettie had taken a photo that showed a strange figure in the background. He went to get her camera.

"This might help you, Sheriff," Jacob said when he returned. The sheriff studied the photo. The figure appeared to be some kind of hairy beast. It was standing at the edge of the forest.

"I can't say for sure what this is," the sheriff said. Then he looked at Ed. "But it's a fact that your daughter was attacked last night. I can assure you that we'll do our best to figure this out."

"There's something else, Sheriff," Jacob said. "A man was here yesterday. He said his name was Siskin. Maybe you've seen him around. Curly gray hair and a red beard?

He was upset about people being in these mountains. Then he told us some wild story about UFOs. They were landing here. He even described the aliens. I think he was trying to scare us off. Do you know who he is?"

The sheriff thought for a few seconds. Then he shook his head. "Doesn't sound familiar." He turned to leave. Ed walked him to his car. "I'll keep you updated on anything I find out, Mr. Marin."

"Thanks. I appreciate that." Dad walked back to the RV. By now the family had packed up all their gear. "Let's get out of here," he said.

It was a short drive to the camping site owned by the Wards. Dad had rented a space for their RV. This way they could enjoy the rest of their vacation. They'd be safe with all the other people around, he thought.

Kyle was there to help them get set up. "That must have been a horrible experience," Kyle said to Lettie. "I'm glad you're okay.

It's too bad that you were forced out of that beautiful spot. But at least you're safe."

Lettie nodded. Ed put his arm around his daughter. "How about we get something to eat," he said.

Inside the restaurant, Lettie and Kyle sat together at their own table. They drank coffee and talked about everything that had been happening.

"The thing that grabbed me had incredible strength. And it was so huge and hairy," Lettie said. "It didn't seem human. Do you think it could have been Bigfoot? Or something like that?" she asked.

Kyle thought carefully before he spoke. He didn't want Lettie to think he doubted her story. "Someone definitely grabbed you, Lettie. I believe that. But no. I don't think there's a half-human, half-ape lurking in these mountains. It has to be some kind of joke. Somebody is dressing up in a gorilla suit and scaring people."

Lettie was shaking her head. "There has to be more to it," she said. "First the people before us were scared away. Then it was my family. What is it about that campsite? Does someone just want it for themselves? Or maybe they're trying to send a message. No campers are welcome here."

"I've talked to a lot of people who live around here," Kyle said. "And you're right. Many have told me they don't like campers coming here. They think all the activity is destroying the wilderness. In their minds it's just getting worse. Every summer there seem to be more people.

"They dump their trash in the rivers and lake," Kyle continued. "A lot of animals get hurt or die because of it. Their heads get stuck in food containers. Some eat plastic, thinking it's food. Or they get tangled up in fishing line or plastic shopping bags. To some of the locals it seems that visitors just don't care. They don't respect nature.

And every year there seem to be fewer animals."

Lettie could hear the passion in Kyle's voice. "Are you one of those people who doesn't like campers coming here?" she asked.

"I love the mountains," Kyle said. "Of course I don't want to see the land trashed. But I love the fact that people can come here and enjoy themselves. It's a special place. I only wish that more people were considerate." Suddenly his mood changed. He smiled at Lettie. "I've got an idea," he said. "We can hike to the lookout point. It has a view of your old campsite. We'll check it out and see if there's any action."

"That would be great," Lettie said. "I'd love to see if anyone—or anything—is there. A strange man tried to scare us off yesterday. His name was Siskin. He was talking about UFOs. Maybe he's there right now talking to an alien." She laughed. But it seemed Kyle hadn't heard her. He was thinking about something.

"Siskin?" Kyle said. "That's the name of a type of bird. The pine siskin. There used to be huge flocks of them. Hundreds of birds would be in a single tree. But now it seems there are less and less of them." He looked at Lettie. "Sorry," he said. "What were you saying? It was something about UFOs."

"Never mind," Lettie said. "Let's tell my parents about the hike."

Dad didn't seem happy about the plan. He frowned and shook his head. "It's too much of a risk, Lettie," he said. "You might be putting yourself in danger. There's been enough of that already. First Jacob was attacked. Then you were dragged off—"

Kyle interrupted. "You have my word, Mr. Marin. Nothing will happen. The Osprey Trail is out in the open and really safe. It's a quick hike up. We'll look around. And then we'll be right back down. I promise we won't do anything risky. I'll take good care of Lettie."

"All right," Dad said. "I guess it's okay."

Lettie had noticed the tone of Kyle's voice. It seemed like he really cared about her. Could it be that he liked her as much as she liked him?

Chapter 8

Everything was set for the hike up Osprey Trail. Lettie and Kyle set off with their backpacks and hiking sticks. Soon Lettie could see that Kyle had been right. The trail wasn't remote at all. There were signs all along the path. Each one told about the wildlife in the area or gave some historical fact.

"Look, Kyle. The sign says this path was part of the Emigrant Trail. The first wagon trains passed through here from the Sierra Nevadas. That was in 1845," Lettie said.

"That's right," he said. "Hundreds of thousands of farmers and gold-seekers were coming to California. It was the most people to move from one area to another in American history."

"Maybe some of the gold-seekers buried their treasure down at our old campsite," Lettie said with a smile.

"I don't think so," Kyle said. "Any miner lucky enough to find gold kept it, I'm sure."

The view from the trail was stunning. Lettie was thrilled to see hawks soaring through the sky. She could also see snow in spots on the mountain that were shaded from the sun.

Finally they were at the lookout point. Kyle took out two pairs of binoculars. He handed one to Lettie. "Look down there," he said, pointing to the campsite. "No one is there. But I can see that your family left it in really good condition. It looks like no one was ever there," he said.

"That's because of Dad," Lettie said. "He taught us certain rules. We always clean up our campsite. That's so the next people can enjoy it."

"I'm impressed," Kyle said. Lettie saw

that he was holding a map. She moved over beside him to look.

The map showed every campsite in the area. Only one was completely private with a close-up view of Owl Lake. The others were clustered in groups together. Lettie could see why someone would be jealous and want the good site for themselves. But the idea of hurting people to get it? That seemed crazy. "Why would someone have wanted us out of there, Kyle?"

"I'm not sure. But they went to the extreme of attacking you, Lettie. That's serious," Kyle said. "And it makes me really mad that anyone would hurt you."

"You're sweet, Kyle. Do you care this much about all the campers?"

"Of course not," Kyle said. "Just the ones with pretty daughters." He smiled at her. Then he laughed. "Actually, I do try to make friends with visitors. They're more likely to take good care of the campground."

Lettie looked through the binoculars again. What she saw surprised her. Two men were moving into the campsite. "Look, Kyle!"

"Hey. I recognize them. They had that spot before. Remember how I told you about the guys with the beat-up car? Then they left. And the family before you got the spot."

Lettie was watching the men through the binoculars. They were busy setting up camp. She had the feeling that they weren't nice people. Something about their faces scared her. Maybe it was because they looked so serious.

Kyle was surveying the entire area. "Well, there's no sign of Bigfoot anyway," he said.

"I wonder how those guys knew to return for the campsite," Lettie said. "We were signed up for a full week. They must have been hanging around somewhere. Just waiting to grab the spot if we moved out. Hey, Kyle. You don't think …"

Kyle looked again at the men. Now

they were using binoculars too. "I think they know we're watching them, Lettie. They're looking in our direction. Somehow we got their attention. Maybe the sun was reflecting off our binoculars. They can't be too happy right now, knowing someone is spying on them."

"Let's head back," Lettie said nervously.

"Wait! I just remembered something," Kyle said. "My grandfather once told me a story about something that happened here. There was this guy who robbed an armored car. He'd gotten away with a million dollars. Before getting caught, he put the money in four boxes. And then he hid them somewhere in the area.

"His plan was to come back for the money when he got out of prison. But he died there. This was about fifty years ago. The story has become a legend. But now I'm wondering if those guys down there know something. Maybe they somehow found a map. What if the money is buried at that campsite?"

"Come on, Kyle. Let's go back," Lettie said.

"Okay." He took another look through the binoculars. "Something's happening, Lettie. One of the guys is still looking up at us. But the other one is at the car. He's reaching inside. Now he's turning around. He's holding … a gun!

"These guys are dangerous," he said. "They could try to chase us if they know the trails. This could be bad, Lettie."

Chapter 9

Is there another path we can take?" Lettie asked, wanting to cry.

"No. This trail is the only way back to the cabins," he said. "Those guys could be headed this way right now. We wouldn't make it even halfway down before they cornered us."

Lettie felt numb. She wasn't sure these were the attackers. But if they were? They'd already taken a lot of risks. Clearly they had a plan and nothing would stop them. They'd probably do anything to get that million dollars.

"What are we going to do, Kyle?" she asked softly.

"We can't risk running into them.

These guys are even more dangerous than Bigfoot," Kyle said. "We'll have to cut across the mountain. There's no trail. Only rocks. But it's the only way."

Lettie nodded. Soon they had left the trail and were climbing over boulders. Instead of heading south toward the cabins, they were heading east. At some point they would head south again.

"We'll end up right behind the cabins," Kyle assured Lettie. "And those guys we'll never see us. But this won't be easy. Are you going to be okay?"

By now Lettie knew her only hope was to trust Kyle. She would have to be brave. "Sure," she said, trying to sound confident. "I hike all the time." That was not exactly true. The hikes she had been on were easy. There was always a nice, neat path.

Lettie followed Kyle as they clawed their way over huge granite boulders. At times they had to crawl. Lettie's knees and elbows were scraped and bleeding a little from the jagged rocks. She didn't say anything to Kyle, though. They just had to get through this.

It seemed like they were making progress. Then Kyle stopped suddenly. "Oh great," he said, looking down.

"What is it?" Lettie asked. She looked in the direction of his gaze. There was water far below them. It was running through a kind of canyon. But it wasn't wide at all.

"You mean we have to go across?" Lettie groaned.

"There's no other way to go," Kyle said. "We could use a rope to swing across."

"Are you crazy?" she cried out. "I said I hike. I'm not into extreme mountain climbing. What if I fall? I could very easily drown. Look how fast that water is moving. Or I could fall on a rock and die."

"Somehow we have to get across, Lettie. Those guys are on their way up the trail right now. They might come this way, looking for us. Then we'll be stuck. Do you want them to push us off this mountain?" Kyle asked.

"But I can't swing across the river," Lettie insisted. "I just can't!"

"Yes you can, Lettie," Kyle said. "I've got a harness and a climbing rope in my backpack. It'll be easy to swing across. It's not that far. Only about six feet."

"I'll fall. I know I will," she said.

Suddenly Kyle's face changed. He looked angry. "So, you're a coward?" Kyle said. His voice was harsh. "I'm not surprised. Most girls are. That's why they can't compete with guys." Kyle didn't mean what he was saying. He was just trying to make Lettie mad enough to lose her fear.

"I am not a coward!" she shouted. Her fear had turned to anger. "Fine. I'll do it. But it will be all your fault if I drown, Kyle Ward!"

Kyle climbed a tree and secured one end of the rope to a limb. Then he tied the other end of the rope to the harness. He handed it to Lettie, and she put it on. Then she backed up to get a good running start.

"You can do it, Lettie!"

Lettie ran as fast as she could. Then she leaped, stretching her front leg out as far as possible. She held her breath as she flew over the water. Lettie landed, letting go of the rope and rolling in the grass. She quickly removed the harness and tossed it back to Kyle. In another minute, he had landed safely beside her.

"Let's go!" Kyle said.

A feeling of elation had come over her. It was hard for her to believe what she'd just done. She had faced a huge challenge and gotten through it. Now the two guys after Lettie and Kyle couldn't reach them. But they kept running until they were back at the cabins.

Lettie's family was waiting with the sheriff. Kyle told them what had happened.

He said that one of the men had a gun. These were probably the guys who had been scaring the Marins.

It wasn't long before the sheriff had found the men. They both had criminal records. In their possession was a map. It was just as Kyle's grandfather had said. The map showed the location of the million dollars. And in one of the men's backpacks was a gorilla suit. They also had a CD of sound effects, including the sounds of shrieking.

◆ ◆ ◆

Later the sheriff joined the Marin family at the restaurant. "It's not likely that we'll find any money buried around here," he said. "I'm pretty sure those fools were chasing after some fake treasure. But at least we know that the mountains are safe. There are no real monsters running around."

"We have a few more days of vacation,"

Dad said. "We could go back to our campsite."

Mom looked worried. "I don't know," she said. "I think I'd like to stay here."

"Well, kids," their father said. "The bad guys are gone now. Should we at least hike down there and look around?"

"Sure. Why not?" Jacob said.

Lettie asked Kyle to come with them. They held hands as they walked. Kyle told her he was sorry for yelling at her earlier. He hadn't meant it. It was okay, Lettie told him. She had realized what he was trying to do.

Now the sun was setting. The sky was quickly getting dark. "Look," Jacob said. "There's something really bright in the sky."

"It's probably just a plane," Dad said, looking up.

The campsite was now just a few feet away. Lettie noticed a figure standing there. It was Siskin! He was looking up at the sky, focused on the bright light. For a second Lettie imagined it was a UFO. Siskin was somehow communicating with it. The thought gave her chills. Of course she didn't believe in UFOs. But something made her stop. "Let's not go any closer," she said. "Let's go back to the RV."

"Why, Lettie?" Jacob asked.

"This is such a beautiful spot. I think we should leave it alone."

"That sounds good to me," Dad said.

It had been a very long day, and everyone was tired. They turned and walked back toward the cabins. The sounds and smells of nature were all around them. They never looked back.

Comprehension Questions

Recall

1. The Marin family planned the camping trip as a family celebration. What two events were they celebrating?

2. Jacob took a walk the first night they were in camp. What was he hoping to see?

Analyzing Characters

1. Which two words could describe Jacob?
   - *knowledgeable*
   - *timid*
   - *environmentalist*

2. Which two words could describe Kyle?
   - *superstitious*
   - *friendly*
   - *resourceful*

Vocabulary

1. What did Mr. Marin mean when he used the word *farfetched* to describe the story the previous campers had given the sheriff?

2. What is meant by an *isolated* campsite?

3. Lettie couldn't believe that something sinister could happen in such a peaceful setting. What does *sinister* mean?

Drawing Conclusions

1. What conclusion did Siskin draw about the holes that had been dug around the Marins' campsite?

2. What conclusion did the Marins draw about Siskin?

3. What conclusion did Lettie come to when she was dragged into the woods?